The Boy with the Magic Numbers

The Boy with the Magic Numbers

Sally Gardner

Orion
Children's Books

ORION CHILDREN'S BOOKS

First published in Great Britain in 2003 by Dolphin Paperbacks
Reissued in 2013 by Orion Children's Books
This edition published in 2016 by Hodder and Stoughton

5 7 9 10 8 6 4

Text and illustrations copyright © Sally Gardner, 2003

The moral rights of the author/illustrator have been asserted.

A CIP catalogue record for this book
is available from the British Library.

ISBN 978 1 4440 1166 1

Printed and bound in Great Britain
by Clays Ltd, St Ives plc

The paper and board used in this book are
made from wood from responsible sources.

MIX
Paper from
responsible sources
FSC® C104740

Orion Children's Books
An imprint of
Hachette Children's Group
Part of Hodder and Stoughton
Carmelite House
50 Victoria Embankment
London EC4Y 0DZ

An Hachette UK Company
www.hachette.co.uk

www.hachettechildrens.co.uk

The present that Dad had left for Billy Pickles was placed under the note that he had stuck to his barber's shop mirror. It said simply, "My number came up and it wasn't the right one. Sorry."

The present was a money-box shaped like the top half of a man. It had a large smiley face and its two hands were folded over its chubby tummy. Billy wondered where the money went in. He couldn't see a slot. It said on the box BATTERIES NOT INCLUDED.

Mum and Billy stood together in the gathering gloom of the barber's shop. They looked at the money-box for a long time, hoping that it might tell them why Dad had gone, and where.

Neither of them spoke and neither of them turned on the lights. They were both looking for clues in the darkness, but everything was just as it had always been. There were the barber's chairs standing in a row, the TV fish tank with its tropical fish swimming aimlessly round and round, the wall covered with framed pictures of Italy and Mighty Mamma.

It was Billy who noticed that Dad's favourite signed photograph was missing. When Mum saw the gap on the wall she let out a little gasp. Dad had taken with him the picture of his hero, the King of Swing, Mr Frank Sinatra.

Billy walked over to the CD player and turned it on. Immediately, Frank Sinatra sang out loud and clear, full of energy and hope:

"New York, New York!"

"I think your dad's gone for good this time, Billy," Mum said softly, turning the music off.

Billy picked up his present and said, "Where do you put the money in?"

"I'm not sure, love," said Mum. "We'll have a proper look at it when we get home. I think we both need a nice cup of tea."

2

Dad's leaving had the same effect as a stone when it is thrown into a pond. The ripples in the water spread out, upsetting everything. Under the stairs, Mum discovered twenty-seven boxes of unopened bills. Before she could do anything about them, the bailiffs turned up and took away the car and the TV.

"Why are they doing that?" asked Billy.

"Your dad liked what he called a flutter on the horses. He bet more money than he had," said Mum. She sighed. "The bailiffs are taking away whatever's valuable so that they can get some of the money back again."

Over the next few months, nearly all the furniture disappeared and Billy and Mum had to put their little house on the market. They moved into rented rooms just above the barber's shop.

Mum was not going to be defeated. It wasn't the first time Dad had gone off without saying a word. But this time it had the feeling of being final. She left her job to take over Dad's barber's shop and put a new notice in the window. It said 'Lily's Unisex Haircuts'.

Dad's regular customers were disappointed not to have Tony cutting their hair and giving them the latest racing tips. They liked listening to Tony's tales. "He'll be back," they said, but when Mum told them just how much Dad owed they had nothing more to say.

Mum's lady customers weren't keen on having their hair done in a barber's chair, so keeping it all going took the roses out of Mum's cheeks.

Billy put the money-box on his window-sill. He would look at it, wondering what it would do if it worked. The instructions said it took Double B batteries and that it only

accepted American dimes. No one in their
small town had ever heard of Double B
batteries and Billy hadn't a penny, let alone
a dime.

"Never mind, love," said Mum. "It was
the thought that counted."

So Dad's thought stayed on Billy's
window-sill, reminding him of all he had
lost.

3

What Billy missed most about his dad was the stories he told of Italy and Mighty Mamma. Dad, who had been christened Antonio Piccoloni, had been the baby of the family. His older brother, Santo, had left home by the time he was born.

"You see, Billy," Dad would laugh, "I wanted Mamma all for myself."

His childhood was a golden time when he dreamed of owning a chain of barbers' shops all over the world. When he grew up, he came to England to make his dream come true. This was how he met Lily, Billy's mum, at a hairdressers' convention in Harrogate.

"The only beautiful woman outside Italy, so what could I do?" And as he said this, he would lift his shoulders and put on a sad face like a clown. "I had to stay and become Tony Pickles."

This always made Billy laugh.

"One day, Billy, when my number comes up, you and me are going to travel. We will visit Mighty Mamma and go see my brother Santo's ice cream café in New York. What you say?"

Billy couldn't wait. Although Dad had never been to New York, his stories of the city were better than fairy tales. New York, according to Dad, was like a magical castle built out of skyscrapers, where in the streets far below the yellow taxi dragons did battle. It was a place where a dreamer could become a king.

About a month after Dad had gone, a postcard arrived. It had a picture of the Statue of Liberty on it and it said

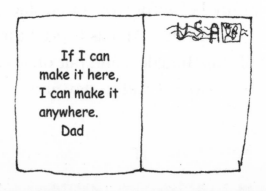

If I can
make it here,
I can make it
anywhere.
Dad

Mum stuck it in the gap where the picture of Frank Sinatra had been.

Billy tried not to think about his dad, but it was hard when there was so much he wanted to ask him. All the questions began with a why. Why did he go off like that without saying a word? Why had he left Mum? Why had he left everything in such a mess?

The trouble was, Billy didn't know how to get hold of Dad to ask him.

"New York's a big place, Billy," said Mum.

"He might be at Uncle Santo's," said Billy hopefully. Mum asked International Directory Enquiries for their help to find the number, but Santo's ice cream café in New York wasn't listed.

"Maybe he'll write soon," said Mum.

Paper kites, that's what Dad's stories were. No more than paper kites, blown away with the wind.

Billy now spent most of his time after

school helping Mum in the barber's shop. They were a team. Mum hadn't enough money to change it into a proper hairdressing salon, but at least the old customers hadn't left her, and because she was so good she soon had some new ones.

Dad's customers missed his horse-racing tips, but Mum had another trick up her sleeve. Her mother had taught her to read the future in the tea leaves. It was an art form, she told Billy.

Mum wasn't sure how good she was at it but the customers weren't complaining. There was now a steady flow of people coming and going all day.

"Better make me look extra smart tonight, Lily," the ladies would say, "if you're right about that tall handsome man."

In the evening Billy would sit with Mum and neatly write down all the money she had made in a little cash book.

"Oh, Billy boy, you make those numbers look magical!" said Mum with pride.

Yet in spite of all Mum's hard work, they were unable to do more than keep their heads above water.

Mum had a little feeling that something was about to change. She'd seen it in the tea leaves. But neither she nor Billy could have imagined just how much, nor that it would have something to do with Mighty Mamma and the money-box.

4

A letter from Dad had arrived at the
beginning of the Easter holidays. In it was a
small cheque for Mum and a ticket to New
York for Billy. Dad wanted him to come
out and stay so that he could meet Mighty
Mamma. She was coming over from Italy
for the seventieth birthday party that Uncle
Santo was giving for her.

Billy was so excited. He had never
travelled further than Lytham St Anne's.
This would be an adventure.

"You won't be upset if I go, Mum?" said
Billy, looking at his mum's pale face.

"No," said Mum. "I think it's a good idea
if Dad answers all your why questions
himself."

A week later Billy was sitting on a plane
flying to the other side of the world, all by
himself. He was seated next to a plump

boy about his own age, dressed in school uniform.

"Hi," said the boy. "I'm Walter Minks Junior."

"I'm Billy Pickles," said Billy, trying to figure out how you worked the video.

Walter leant over to help.

"Are you flying on your own too?" said Billy.

"Yes, I fly all the time. I go to boarding school in Sussex and come home to the States every holiday."

Billy and Walter got on well, and talking

17

and playing cards made the journey go by faster.

"Do you live in New York?" asked Billy.

"Yep. Nope. I spend half the holidays with my dad in New York and the other half with my mum in Hollywood," said Walter.

Billy showed him the address Dad had sent him.

"You're not that far away from my dad," said Walter. "Look, why don't I give you my number and I'll take yours, and maybe we can meet up?"

"I'd like that," said Billy.

An air steward saw the two boys through immigration and out into a wave of waiting people. It seemed to Billy that he had landed on another planet. Everything was whirling around him. He couldn't see Dad anywhere.

"Who's meeting you boys?" asked the steward.

"My driver," said Walter.

"My dad," said Billy with pride.

A very smart man stepped forward.

"That's him," said Walter. "Hope to see you again, Billy." And he faded into the crowd.

Billy stood there, feeling suddenly very alone and wondering where his dad could be. The steward said kindly, "Don't worry, Billy. The traffic out of New York can be bad. I'm sure your dad will be here soon."

"Billy!" Someone was shouting. "Billy!"

Billy looked round, but he couldn't see anyone he knew. Then the crowds parted and before him stood a small elderly lady not much taller than himself. She had a pretty face and dark brown eyes.

"Billy Pickles! Oh, how good to see you! I knew it was you. You look just like your nonno, my late husband Alfredo." She gave Billy two kisses on each cheek.

Billy looked startled.

"You don't know who I am? I am Mighty

Mamma, your nonna, your grandmother."

Billy had always imagined Mighty Mamma to be well mighty. Not tiny and frail. The only pictures he had ever seen of her were the photographs on Dad's shop wall, all taken when she was very young and beautiful. Although she wasn't at all how Billy had imagined her, he knew straight away he liked her.

"Excuse me," said the steward, "but Billy's dad is supposed to be meeting him."

Mighty Mamma huffed. "So? He couldn't make it. I am here." And she handed the steward a letter.

"OK, everything's in order," said the steward, reading the letter. "Are you going to be all right, Billy?"

Billy nodded and said, "Fine."

"Santo!" shouted Mighty Mamma. "Over here!"

Billy looked up to see a mountain of a man coming towards them with a trolley and a beaming face.

"Mighty Mamma, he looks just like Pappa," said Santo. "Forgive us, Billy. Nice to meet you." He held out a huge friendly hand. "And welcome to the Big Apple."

"Where's Dad?" asked Billy when they were all packed into a taxi.

"He's tied up in a meeting," said Santo quickly, giving the taxi driver instructions. "Take the Williamsburg Bridge please, not the tunnel."

Somehow, Billy got the feeling that neither Mighty Mamma nor Uncle Santo was too pleased with Dad.

5

Santo's apartment was small and cosy with lots of pictures on the walls, just like Dad's barber's shop. Billy was looking at them when the doorbell rang. Uncle Santo went to answer it. A lady walked into the lounge. She had bright pink hair and looked just like a piece of candyfloss on a stick.

"Oh sugar!" squeaked the lady. "You must be Tony's boy! He looks like Tony's boy, don't you think?"

She walked up to Billy and pinched his cheek. Under her arm she was carrying a little dog wearing a pink jumper that matched her own.

"This is Miss Precious. She's a chihuahua. Don't you think she's a cutiepie?"

Miss Precious let out a piercing yap, showing a set of very sharp little teeth.

Mighty Mamma came out of the kitchen carrying a tray. "What are you doing here, Trixie?" she said sharply.

"It's just that Tony would like to see his son, and I thought I could kinda take him over to the apartment and, like, we could all get acquainted."

"Do you know my dad, then?" said Billy, surprised.

"You betcha, sweetiepie. Why, your dad and me are . . ."

"Coffee, Billy?" interrupted Mighty Mamma.

"No thanks, Mrs Piccoloni, it gives me tummy trouble," said Trixie.

"I wasn't asking you," said Mighty Mamma. "I think it's best you go. Santo will bring Billy along after he has had a little rest."

Whether it was the jetlag or whether it was because he was in a strange place, Billy wasn't sure, but he felt as if he was trying to put a jigsaw puzzle together with half the pieces missing.

As soon as Trixie had gone Billy asked Mighty Mamma, "Am I staying with you or with Dad?"

She took Billy's hands. "That's up to you," she said. "Why don't you see what you think when you've seen your dad?"

Dad's apartment was over a dry-cleaning shop and was nowhere near as nice or as cosy as Uncle Santo's. A familiar sound of yap-yapping could be heard coming from another room. Dad looked different somehow. He was trimmer.

"Good to see your old dad or what?" he said, flinging his arms round Billy and trying to lift him off the ground. "You're too big," he said, putting on his sad clown face. "First your babies break your arms, then your children break your heart."

Billy laughed. "I'm not a baby any more, Dad."

"I know, I know. Well, what do you think of New York? Isn't it just the ticket?"

Billy felt as if his dad was putting on a show for his and Uncle Santo's benefit. He hadn't asked Billy about Mum once.

A door opened and out came Trixie and Miss Precious. The dog was yapping away,

this time dressed in a purple jumper with a
bow on the top of her head.

"It's good to see you again, kid," said
Trixie. "Hey, didn't I tell you, Tony? He's
the spitting image of you!"

Dad looked a little sheepish. "Yeah," he
said. "Why don't you go and fix Santo a
beer, Trixie?"

"It can wait," said Trixie, putting her
arms round Dad's neck and kissing him.

Billy felt angry. What was this candyfloss lollipop doing, hanging on to his dad like a brooch? Trixie looked at Billy and then at Tony. Dad seemed embarrassed.

"Well, are you going to tell him, honey, or shall I?" said Trixie, fluttering her long eyelashes.

"I think we should wait until Billy's settled in," said Dad, brushing her off. "He's only just arrived. Give the kid a chance."

"Tell me what?" said Billy angrily.

There was an awkward silence. Then Trixie squeaked, "I'm going to be your new stepmom."

6

Billy had not wanted to stay at Dad's after that. His stomach suddenly felt as if it were made out of lead. He knew his mum and dad weren't married but still, it didn't feel right his dad marrying someone else. Not so soon, anyway. And what about him and Mum?

Uncle Santo, seeing tears well up in Billy's eyes, rescued him by saying firmly, "I think the kid's tired. Perhaps this is not the right moment."

With that they left. Outside it was getting dark.

"Could we walk a bit?" asked Billy.

"Sure," said Santo. "Anyway, we'll have more luck getting a cab a couple of blocks up."

The street was busy and it had begun to rain when Billy saw a man standing in the doorway of a shop. He was dressed in a long patched raincoat and perched on the top of his head he wore a toy witch's hat tied on with a piece of string. He smiled at Billy and said, "You want Double B batteries?"

Billy stopped and went over to look in the man's tray. It was full of batteries, all out of their wrappers. Each had written on them in spidery writing what they were, AAAAA batteries, CC batteries and so on. Billy couldn't see any Double B batteries anywhere.

"They're a dollar each," said the man.

"Have you really got Double B batteries?" said Billy.

"Yep," said the man. "Those are mighty special batteries. I don't put them on show for everybody, or else they would have all gone by now."

Billy had been given twenty one-dollar bills by Mum "just in case", and this was a just in case moment if ever there was one.

"No, Billy," said Uncle Santo, taking his hand and walking him away. "There are a lot of people in this city trying to sell you something. Just take no notice. Come on, I don't want you getting lost."

"Please," said Billy, pulling him back. "Dad gave me a money-box and it needs a Double B battery. I've got a dollar."

Uncle Santo was about to say there was no such thing as a Double B battery, but the look on Billy's face melted his heart.

"OK," he said, "but don't be too upset if it doesn't work."

"You're in luck," said the man, handing Billy the battery. "I've been keeping this one back because it's so powerful. I hope it brings you what you want."

On the battery were the words Double B and in tiny faint writing "Not Long Life".

When they got back to Santo's apartment, Mighty Mamma had cooked a huge bowl of pasta.

"I'm sorry, Billy," said Mighty Mamma. "Santo, he tell me what happened. This is all very upsetting. It's very hard sometimes to understand why grown-ups make such silly mistakes."

Billy was feeling better and very sleepy now that he had eaten. It had been a long day. So much had happened, so much that he didn't understand.

Mighty Mamma tucked him up in bed.

"Oh," said Billy. "My battery. I didn't . . . " but before he could finish what he was saying, Billy Pickles was fast asleep.

7

In the morning Billy got out of bed, unpacked his money-box carefully from his rucksack, put in the battery and turned it on. The smiling mouth opened and a tongue shot out. It seemed a little disappointing if that was all it did, especially after it had taken him so long to find the right battery. He read the instructions again and saw that they said: "Place a dime on the tongue".

Mighty Mamma was sitting in front of the TV when Billy asked her if he could have a dime to put in his money-box.

"No good morning? Just dimes?" said Mighty Mamma.

"Oh, I'm sorry. Good morning. It's just . . ." and Billy told Mighty Mamma all about Dad's present and how he and Santo had found a man selling Double B batteries.

"Eh!" said Mighty Mamma, after hearing

Billy's tale, "I would like to see where my dime goes."

Billy brought the money-box into the lounge and placed it on the table near the TV. He put the dime on the tongue and it disappeared. They heard the coin clink. Then the money-box rubbed its tummy with one hand whilst holding the other out in front.

"I have never seen a money-box like that. What do you think it wants?" said Mighty Mamma. "Here, put another dime on its hand. Let's see if it does anything."

Billy did this and the hand threw the money into the money-box's mouth. Both Billy and Mamma were delighted.

"Well, who would have thought they could make a money-box do that! What will they think of next?" said Mighty Mamma.

They were both getting up to go into the kitchen to make some breakfast when the money-box spoke. It said, "562."

Billy went over to the money-box. "What did you say?"

The money-box said it again. "562."

"What does it mean?" said Mighty Mamma.

"I don't know," said Billy.

"Do you want another two dimes to see if it does it again?"

Billy took the dimes from his grandmother, but then he remembered what was written on the battery, "Not Long Life", so he turned the money-box off and put the dimes on the table. He would show it to his dad later.

Billy had breakfast and got dressed and forgot all about his talking money-box. Much more important was the fact that his dad was going to pick him up and show him New York. He couldn't wait. He would have a chance to talk to Dad properly and ask him all his "why" questions.

At one o'clock Dad still hadn't shown up. Billy sat on the sofa waiting with Mighty Mamma and watching the Katy Gee Guessing Game show.

"Now, my friends," said Katy Gee, "today we have the most yummy chocolate chip cake and your guess, viewers, is this. How many chocolate chips are in the cake? The prize for the lucky winner is a Magic Fix blender and there's a bonus prize if you get the number spot on. So what are you waiting for? The lines are now open."

"Where is Tony?" said Mighty Mamma. "He should have been here three hours ago."

"Why don't we phone up and say the money-box number?" said Billy.

Mighty Mamma looked at him. "Sorry about your dad, Billy. I will have strong words with him when he finally gets here."

"Mighty Mamma, please," said Billy. "Can we call the Katy Gee show and say 562 and see if the money-box is right?"

8

An hour later Billy and Mighty
Mamma were being driven to
the TV studios downtown to
pick up their prize in person.
The money-box had got the
number spot on.

Katy Gee was delighted to
see Billy and his grandma. "This
is truly wonderful, Mrs
Piccoloni. How did you guess
the right number?"

"It was my grandson," said
Mighty Mamma. She put an
arm round Billy. "He has a way
with the numbers." The
audience clapped.

"And this is the first time you have been
to New York?" said Katy Gee.

"Yes," said Billy.

The audience clapped again.

"What have you seen so far?"

"Your show and the view from a taxi,"

said Billy. "This is my first day."

"Billy Pickles," said Katy Gee, "we are about to change all that. The bonus prize is a ride for four people over Manhattan in a helicopter."

"Wow!" said Billy.

After the show was over they were taken on a tour of the studios. Then they had lunch with Katy Gee. She still could not get over how clever Billy and Mighty Mamma had been.

"You have no idea," she said, "how rare it is for anyone to get the number spot on. How did you do it?"

"It's our little secret," said Mighty Mamma, looking at Billy.

The day ended with a stretch limo driving them back to the apartment.

"Makes up a little for Dad not showing, eh?" said Mighty Mamma as they drove up Fifth Avenue.

"A little," said Billy, smiling.

9

Mighty Mamma and Billy put the Magic Fix blender on the kitchen table next to the yummy-looking chocolate cake from the studio.

"What's this, Mamma?" said Santo when he got home that afternoon.

"It is a present to you from Billy and me," said Mighty Mamma with a cheeky smile on her face.

"No, you shouldn't have, Mamma. There is no need," said Santo. "This machine is very expensive. You can't afford to go getting me presents, Mamma."

"I wish I could have bought it for you, Santo, but the truth is I didn't," said Mighty Mamma mysteriously.

"Then how come it's here if you didn't buy it?" said Santo.

"Go on, guess how many chocolate chips are in that cake," said Billy.

Santo scratched his head. "I don't know," he said, laughing.

"Go on," said Billy. "Guess."

"All right then, 283," said Santo.

"No," said Mighty Mamma, "there are 562 exactly!" Then she and Billy told him how they had won the blender and all about their extraordinary day. Santo was most impressed.

"How did you guess the right number?"

"It was the battery I bought," said Billy.

"No, it can't be," laughed Santo. "Anyway, Billy, who are you going to take on this helicopter ride?"

Billy said without a second thought, "I would like to take Mighty Mamma, and you and my friend Walter."

"What about your dad?" said Santo.

Billy shook his head. "Not Dad," he said. "He might not show up."

10

That evening Dad and Trixie turned up to take Billy out for a meal. Mighty Mamma was waiting for them in the hall. She took Dad by the ear, dragged him into the kitchen and shut the door. For the first time Billy caught a glimpse of why the word mighty went with Mamma. She sounded like a machine gun firing words off rat-a-tat-tat in Italian.

"It's a good thing we don't understand what they're saying," said Trixie, who was sitting on the sofa adjusting Miss Precious's leopardskin jacket and diamante collar. "Do you see, honey," she said to Billy, "how she matches my coat and my engagement ring? Don't we both look a picture?"

Billy said nothing. He wished he had been taught Italian. After a few minutes Dad came into the room, the smile wiped off his face.

"Are you ready, Billy?" said Mighty Mamma. "Your dad's taking you out to a restaurant."

"Oh gee whizz, I sure could do with

something to eat," said Trixie, jumping up.

"No," said Mighty Mamma firmly. "Not you. I think Tony has some explaining to do to Billy first."

"I'm sure I could help," said Trixie, but one look at Mighty Mamma's face told her she would be eating alone.

Dad took Billy to a restaurant a few blocks away. They didn't speak much. Billy could see that Mighty Mamma's words were still whooshing around Dad's head, but he had recovered by the time they were seated and had ordered their food.

"This was the favourite haunt of Frank Sinatra," said Dad. "What do you think?"

Billy thought that the pastrami sandwich that turned up could have fed him and Mum for a couple of nights.

"Look, kid," said Dad, "I'm sorry. We got off to a bad start, but we're friends, right?"

Billy nodded. His mouth was too full to speak.

Dad looked uncomfortable.

"Billy, I wasn't cut out to be a small town barber in the middle of nowhere. You've got to understand. I have big ideas. Ideas need a city. This, buddy, is a big city, where fortunes are made on no more than a dream. I tell you, I have big dreams and I'm going to make them come true."

"Why did you leave Mum and me?" asked Billy.

Dad ignored what Billy had said and carried on. "I've got me a business partner, a great guy called Nathan Chance. He's Trixie's boss. He's from the big country, you know, where they wear cowboy hats and boots. He thinks my idea's a sure-fire winner and he wants to come in on it with me. Do you want to know what my idea is?"

Billy was looking down at the table. He didn't feel hungry any more. He just wished he was home with Mum.

"Wagon Trail tours!" continued Dad.

"Going along the same route as they did in the days of old but with all mod cons. What do you think?"

Billy sat there feeling unhappy. What had any of this to do with him or Mum?

"Come on, Billy. This is America. Aren't you excited? I'm going to be rich. We're all going to be rich."

"All I want to know," said Billy, fighting back the tears, "is why you left Mum and me and why you're going to marry Trixie."

Dad's ears had started to go red, just like Billy's did when he wasn't telling the truth.

"Your mum and me — how shall I put it? — grew apart. Hey, it happens. But look, kid, the most important thing is that we're here together in a restaurant that Frank Sinatra ate in. Doesn't that make you feel top of the heap? A number one?"

"No," said Billy. "It makes me feel sad."

"Come on! Cheer up. Tonight I'm in the money, so splash out and get yourself a great dessert."

"No thank you," said Billy. "Can we go back to Santo's now?"

"Do you know how many wives Frank Sinatra had?" said Dad, getting the bill.

"What's that got to do with anything?" said Billy.

"Look, kid," said Dad. "There's a lot you don't understand. And I'm sorry but I want to tell you, to get the record straight." He put his hand out to touch Billy's shoulder. Billy moved quickly away.

"See, I love Trixie. She's a great girl and, well, she makes your old dad happy. Just try and be nice to her. She's got such a kind heart."

After that, Billy felt there was no point to his "why" questions. The whys just hung between them, angry and unanswered. Grown-ups, thought Billy, were a mystery.

They made their way back to Santo's apartment in silence.

Mighty Mamma opened the door and one look at Billy's face told her that things hadn't gone well. Billy went and sat in the lounge. He could hear Mighty Mamma saying, "So you will be here tomorrow, Tony, to take Billy out?"

"I can't," said Dad. "I've told you, I have to work. It's important, Mamma, that I get this right. Our future depends on it. I can't look after the kid as well. Come on, please help me out here."

Billy got up and went into his room. He didn't want to listen to any more. He sat on his bed, tears rolling down his face. He said aloud, "I wish I was home with Mum."

The money-box was on the side table and Billy turned it on and put a dime on the tongue. The money-box clanked it down, rubbed its tummy, and threw the other coin into its mouth. Even through his tears it made Billy smile. Then it said 26, 34, 12, 19, 21, 7 and, after another clink, 3. Billy wrote the numbers down and turned off his money-box. He got undressed and into bed.

Mighty Mamma came in with some hot milk and a cookie. She sat on the bed next to Billy.

"Come here and let your old nonna give you a hug," said Mighty Mamma. "This hasn't been easy for you, has it?"

"No," said Billy.

"Sometimes grown-ups are a real disappointment," said Mighty Mamma. "They can be much more selfish and childish than children and that is bad because they are old enough to know better and they don't."

"The money-box came up with some more numbers," said Billy.

"It did?" said Mighty Mamma.

"Yes," said Billy. "I wrote them down." He showed them to Mighty Mamma.

She stared at them and said, "I told Tony to phone your mamma this evening and tell her what's going on."

"Good," said Billy.

They sat on the bed together, looking at the money-box and listening to the hum of New York outside.

"I don't think the numbers can have anything to do with chocolate cake," said Billy after a while.

"I shouldn't think so," said Mighty Mamma. "It would be one giant cake to have so many chocolate chips in it, don't you think?"

Billy went to brush his teeth, then got into bed and snuggled up under the covers.

"I forget to tell you. I called Walter and he would love to come," said Mighty Mamma.

"Great," said Billy. "I wonder what those numbers mean?"

"I don't know, Billy," said Mighty Mamma. "Maybe it was luck that the money-box came up with the right numbers today. Maybe they don't mean anything. Maybe

they do. Who knows?"

She kissed Billy goodnight and turned
off the light. In the darkness of the room,
the money-box smiled at Billy. If only he
knew how amazing those numbers would
prove to be.

11

All Detective Jack Sherman from the New York City Police Department wanted was a quiet day and to get home in time for his daughter's sixth birthday. He certainly didn't want a constant headache over a safe. It had been pulled out of the Hudson River ten days earlier, and so far no one had managed to get it open.

It was not through lack of trying. The safe dated back to a bank robbery that had taken place in the 1920s. There were diamonds worth a small fortune inside. The newspapers had got hold of the story and it had captured the imagination of New Yorkers. Apparently the robbers had been defeated by the safe, and rather than be caught with it they had dumped it in the river. Now it sat in a room surrounded by guards and safe-breakers, none of whom

could get it open.

To make matters worse, the Chief of Police was breathing down Detective Sherman's neck.

"It's making the police department look stupid, not being able to open a safe from the 1920s," he growled.

Jack Sherman took a deep breath and started to explain for the hundredth time that this safe had been made by a master locksmith. He was famous for making the safest safes in the world. There were apparently over a billion combinations. One of those would open the safe, but no one knew which. Detective Sherman had people working round the clock, but still they weren't anywhere nearer to solving the problem.

"I don't want a history lesson," yelled the Chief of Police. "Just get that safe open today. That's an order."

Oh heck, thought Detective Sherman. Weren't there more important things he could be doing than this? Like capturing the fraudster Spike the Spider, for example. This crook had been taking people's money under false pretences for years, but so far he had always managed to get away and pin the blame on someone else.

Jack Sherman was now on his third cup of coffee. He couldn't sit here all day, waiting for someone to break that darned code.

Suddenly he remembered what his wife

had said last night about an English kid with an Italian grandma who had guessed the right number of chocolate chips in a cake. "They got it spot on," she had said, "not just nearly right but one hundred per cent right. Don't you think that's remarkable?"

Detective Sherman picked up the phone. "Get me the Katy Gee show, please," he said.

12

The helicopter took off in a whirl, dipping out over the Hudson and towards the Statue of Liberty. They circled overhead looking down at the golden torch in her hand.

"Oh wow! That's something!" said Walter.

"Look," shouted Billy over the noise of the helicopter. "How small everybody is!"

"This is superb," said Mighty Mamma. "Santo, come look, you will never see your city like this again."

"Hey, Billy," said Santo, looking a little green. "All this for guessing the right number of chocolate chips!"

"Are you all right?" said Billy, seeing the worried look on Uncle Santo's face.

"I don't like heights," said Santo nervously.

They were now flying over Central Park. "I can see where I live," said Walter.

"That's the Dakota Building, home to the

rich and famous," said the pilot.

Billy looked impressed and said, "That must be nice." Walter didn't say anything.

"You wouldn't think Central Park was so big," said Mighty Mamma.

"The green lungs of New York, Mamma," said the pilot.

When they landed, Detective Jack Sherman was waiting at the heliport to greet them.

"Are you Mrs Piccoloni?" said Detective Sherman, holding out a hand towards her.

"What's Tony done now?" said Mighty Mamma.

"Sorry, lady, I don't know who Tony is. I am looking for you and Billy Pickles. I have a problem that you might be able to help me with."

"What's going on?" said Uncle Santo, who was still feeling a little wobbly on his legs. "We've done nothing wrong."

"I know," said the detective. "Look, this

may sound nuts to you, but let me explain."
He told them all about the robbery and the
safe. "It's a gamble," he said. "You might be
able to crack it or you might not. Frankly,
I'm so desperate I'd use smoke signals if I
thought they would work. Will you come
back to the precinct with me?"

Billy looked at Mighty Mamma.

"Excuse me," said Mighty Mamma, "I need to talk to my grandson alone."

They walked a little way off.

"Have you got those numbers?" said Mighty Mamma.

"Yes," said Billy, "but they might be wrong. They might be for something else."

"Billy," said Mighty Mamma. "Like I said last night, this whole thing might mean something or it might mean nothing. So, what have we got to lose?" She shrugged her shoulders just like Dad.

"OK," said Billy. "We could pick up the money-box on the way to the precinct. But what about Walter?"

"Don't worry," said Mighty Mamma. "Santo can take Walter back to the café and we can join them later."

When they arrived at the precinct, Billy and Mighty Mamma were taken to a room full of people and computers. On a table in

the middle sat the safe. A man was
listening to it with a stethoscope.

"It looks like they've all gone mad," Billy
whispered to Mighty Mamma. Detective
Sherman overheard him and laughed.

"Not far from the truth, kid," he said.
"Well, how do you want to work this?"

"How many numbers does it need?"
asked Billy.

"Five," said Detective Sherman.

"Single or double?"

"Single."

"I have to speak to Mighty Mamma alone," said Billy.

They walked over to a corner of the room. Everyone was looking at them.

"Then the numbers you got last night won't work," said Mighty Mamma.

"No," said Billy.

"We need to see if the money-box can give us the right numbers," said Mighty Mamma.

"We'd better put in another dime," said Billy.

"Scusi, we can't work with people watching us," said Mighty Mamma to everyone in the room, "so if you want us to help you, we need to be left alone. Could everyone leave the room, please, and let's see if we can get this thing open."

When everybody had left, Billy put the money-box on the top of the safe and fed it the first dime. The money-box clinked it down and rubbed its tummy. It threw the other dime into its mouth. Then it said: "1 4 7 4 9."

Billy wrote the numbers down carefully on a piece of paper, turned the money-box off and was just putting it away in his rucksack when the door flew open and the Chief of Police came storming in, followed by Detective Sherman.

"Sherman, would you care to tell me

what these people are doing here? This is not a game show," said the Chief of Police.

"I know that, sir, but I thought they just might be able to help," said Detective Sherman.

"Would you like the number?" said Billy.

The Chief of Police snatched the piece of paper from Billy and walked up to the safe. He turned the dial, then pulled at the door. Nothing happened.

"Just as I thought. Sheer waste of time!" thundered the Chief of Police. "Sherman, you've got some explaining to do!"

At that moment there was a loud click and the dial on the front of the safe started spinning round and round. Then the huge door creaked open to reveal its gleaming treasure.

13

By the time Billy and Mighty Mamma had got back to Santo's café, they had already appeared on the early evening news. The boy who cracked the safe was the top story.

Santo got them all an ice cream while they sat watching the TV. The Chief of Police was saying that the breakthrough had been made possible by the superb work of Detective Sherman, who had the brains to think in an imaginative way and get hold of the kid who was good with numbers.

"Did you have a good time here?" said Billy to Walter.

"It's been great," said Walter excitedly. "Santo let me help serve in the café and we sold I don't know how many ice creams."

Mighty Mamma turned away from the TV and looked at Santo. "You didn't make the kid work for you," she said.

"Honestly, Mrs Piccoloni, it was the best day ever," said Walter.

"You know, this kid," said Santo, patting Walter on the back, "could sell ice creams to Iceland. He has the golden touch. I tell you, Mamma, I have never seen it in one so young. You can have a job any time, kid." They all laughed.

Just then the door opened and Trixie came tottering in on very high stiletto heels, accompanied by Miss Precious. Both were dressed in a mixture of greens and reds.

"Why, Billy, I've just seen you on TV!" cried Trixie. "Oh my, aren't you smart! How do you do it?"

"Are you going to sit down or stand there looking like a Christmas tree?" said Mighty Mamma.

Trixie sat down.

"This is Walter, my friend," said Billy. "Walter, this is Trixie. She works for my dad's business partner."

"My pleasure, I'm sure," said Trixie, brushing him aside. "I phoned Tony the minute I saw you and told him the whole story and he says he's coming over right away."

"I've got to go, Mrs Piccoloni. My driver's here," said Walter. "It's been a really great day, the best ever."

"It's been a pleasure, Walter, and you can call me Mighty Mamma," said Mighty Mamma.

"Any time," said Santo. "Any time, you can come and spend the afternoon with me."

"Could you come over to my place tomorrow, Billy? If that's all right with you, Mighty Mamma," said Walter.

"I'd love to," said Billy.

"That's all right with me," said Mighty Mamma.

"Thanks, Mighty Mamma. OK then, Billy, Arnold my driver will pick you up about ten," said Walter.

"That kid has a driver!" said Trixie, turning round to watch Walter leave the café. "You know, I'm sure I've seen him before in some magazine. What's his surname?"

"Minks," said Billy.

Trixie let out a shriek and nearly fell off her chair. "Oh my! I don't believe it! I have actually said hello to Marilyn Tinsel's boy!"

Both Mighty Mamma and Billy looked at Trixie as if she had lost her marbles.

"Are you all right?" said Mighty Mamma.

"Surely you've heard of Marilyn Tinsel? Why, everyone's heard of Marilyn Tinsel," said Trixie, all in a tizz.

"Apparently not," said Santo.

70

"She's in all the papers and magazines!" cried Trixie. "She was married to Walter Minks the Third."

"What are you talking about?" said Mighty Mamma. "Have a drink of water and calm down. Walter is just Billy's friend, that's all."

At that moment Billy's dad came in.

"Where's my boy? Where's the kid who cracked the safe? Two days in New York and you're already a star. What did I tell you, Billy?" He started singing his favourite Frank Sinatra song.

"Enough of Frank Sinatra," said Mighty Mamma.

Dad looked wounded and clutched at his heart. "You can never have enough of Ol' Blue Eyes," he said with feeling. He kissed Mighty Mamma on both cheeks.

"So, kid, tell your old dad the secret. How do you do it?"

"He doesn't," said Mighty Mamma.

Billy's heart gave a lurch. His grandma

wasn't about to give the game away, was she?

"We do it together," said Mighty Mamma. Now if you will excuse us, we are tired and we're going home."

"But I thought we could take Billy out for a meal," said Dad. "You know, paint the town red. What do you say?"

"I say no," said Mighty Mamma. "You were too busy to see your son yesterday. You were too busy to be with him today. Now he has been on TV, you suddenly have time. No," she repeated firmly. "Remember you have work to do. Don't let us keep you from it."

Billy felt pleased that Mighty Mamma had said no. Dad stood there looking hurt as she took Billy firmly by the hand and left.

Back at the apartment, Mighty Mamma made Billy a delicious supper. She laid the table with a checked tablecloth and lit the candles.

"This is like I do it back home when I have guests," said Mighty Mamma.

"It's like a restaurant, only better," said Billy.

Dessert was home-made chocolate profiteroles. It was the best thing Billy had ever tasted.

"Wow!" said Billy. "Thank you, Mighty Mamma."

Mighty Mamma smiled. "Your mum, she brought you up well, Billy. One day I would very much like to meet her."

"I wonder what those other numbers were for?" said Billy, licking the last bit from his spoon.

"I don't understand it," said Mighty Mamma, "but one thing I do know is that those numbers sure mean something. But what they mean — that is another question."

14

The apartment Walter lived in was like a film set. It had marble floors and oak-panelled rooms full of beautiful paintings.

There was even a grand staircase. A butler had let Billy in and a housekeeper had served them lunch.

Walter's room had pictures of pirates painted on the walls and a ceiling with a night sky on it that twinkled when you turned on the light. It was packed full of toys, just like a shop, and half of them were still in their boxes and wrappers. This, thought Billy, was something else, something unreal.

"You have the latest G5 Quantum game," said Billy. "Wow, it costs well — "

Billy stopped what he was saying and looked at Walter. He was sitting on his bed looking miserable.

"It was a bad idea you coming here. Now you'll think I'm a spoilt pig, like all the other kids do."

Billy went and sat next to him. "Don't be daft. I don't think that. I think you're grand."

"What does that mean?" said Walter.

"I think you're all right," said Billy. "It's just amazing to have so many toys and a room with paintings on the wall."

"I'd give them all away to have a family like yours, where you're wanted."

"Oh come on," said Billy. "Look at all this. Of course you're wanted, otherwise you'd have nothing, right?"

"Wrong," said Walter. "My dad's so busy that I have to make an appointment to see him. We always go out to a smart restaurant. He tells his assistant that he won't be taking any calls. We sit there and over lunch I tell him how well I'm doing at school and show him my report. If it's bad I don't get dessert. If his assistant interrupts us while we're having our quality time lunch together he goes ballistic." He pointed at all the unopened toys. "Go on, look at them. They all have stickers on them."

Billy looked and sure enough they all had girls' names written on them.

"Who are they all?" asked Billy.

"My dad's girlfriends. They all give me presents and the ones that are crossed out with a red marker are old girlfriends. You think your dad's bad, but mine is terrible. When we have one of our awful lunches I have to make sure I get the name of his current girlfriend right, otherwise he goes nuts."

"It sounds bad," said Billy. "What about your mum?"

"She's a movie star," said Walter. "She left me when I was five and moved to LA. She married a film director who can't stand children. He says they age stars treble, so I am not allowed to be seen with Mum in public. I stay in a wing of their house away from everybody. They get me the latest games and DVDs, and there's a huge pool to swim in, but I would much rather they wanted to be with me."

"Well," said Billy, "Mum and me haven't

anything apart from — " Billy thought for a
minute — "I mean we're really poor."

"I'd love to have a family like yours,
where you're really wanted and you're not
just a parcel," said Walter.

"Would you like to know a secret?" said
Billy, who didn't like seeing Walter so sad.

79

"You promise you won't tell?"

"Promise," said Walter, cheering up.

Billy told him all about the money-box.

"That's amazing!" said Walter. "I'd love to see it working."

"I'm sure you can next time we meet," said Billy, "but the thing is, it says on the batteries 'Not Long Life', so I have to use it carefully."

15

Dad turned up alone the next day to take Billy out. He brought Mighty Mamma flowers and said he was sorry.

"Are we going up to the top of the Empire State Building?" asked Billy excitedly as they left the apartment.

"No," said Dad, "not today. My business partner, he's keen to meet you and I want to show you my office. What do you say?"

Billy felt it didn't matter what they did as long as it was just him and Dad. They got a cab downtown to his office. Billy's heart sank when they got out of the elevator and saw Trixie waiting for them. She was wearing a genuine cowgirl costume with rhinestones. Miss Precious had a matching outfit with a sheriff's badge.

"Welcome to The Past is Your Present Tours!" said Trixie.

Billy stared at her open-mouthed.

"Guess who I am. Go on," said Trixie.

"I haven't a clue," said Billy, looking bewildered.

"It's so easy you'll kick yourself when I tell you," said Trixie. "It's Annie Get Your Gun, of course!"

Billy sighed. Mighty Mamma had told him not to get his hopes up about today and she couldn't have been more right.

Dad's office was the size of a broom cupboard. By the time all three of them were inside, it was hard to close the door.

"Small and compact, that's the way I like it," said Dad, sitting squashed behind his tiny desk.

"Where's your computer?" asked Billy.

"Don't need one," said Dad. "A mobile phone is all I need, and this." He took out a shoebox. In it was a model of an old-fashioned Wild West wagon.

This all seems to be getting sillier by the minute, thought Billy.

"I told you — we're selling wagon trail tours," said Dad. "So that you can travel like they did in days of old but with all the comforts that the twenty-first century has to offer. You can spend time eating round a campfire and sleeping under the moon and the stars."

"What about the bathroom?" said Trixie. "I mean, no one wants to do you know what in the open."

"The finer details are being worked out as we speak," said Dad grandly. "But every day I get people buying one of our tours. What do you think, kid? Is it good or is it good?"

"When do they start?" said Billy.

"The first one is in a month's time. There's still a lot to do. Exciting, isn't it?" said Dad, beaming.

"But, honey, shouldn't you know what you are going to do about the bathroom by now?" said Trixie.

"Sweetie, don't worry your pretty little head," said Dad. "Tony Pickles has it all under control. There's a team of product designers in Chicago working on the wagons as we speak. Come on, Billy, let me introduce you to my business partner."

Nathan Chance's office was like the man, big. His snakeskin cowboy boots rested on the desk in front of him. His cowboy hat

was pushed back off his face. He wore
shades and was smoking a large cigar and
blowing out smoke rings.

"Howdy, kid," he said, slowly rocking

back and forth in his chair. "Your dad tells me you have a winning way with numbers. So OK, let's see how good you really are. What's nine times eight?"

"I don't know," said Billy.

"OK. Tony, what's the answer?"

"Sorry," said Dad, "it's just slipped right out of my head."

"Well, you're all hopeless and it proves my point. The boy's just had two lucky strikes, that's all," said Nathan.

"Seventy-two," said Trixie. They all turned to look at her.

"Well, I like the outfit, sugar," Nathan said. "OK, boy who's good with numbers, what's the number of the horse that will come in first in the 2.30 today?"

"Don't know," said Billy. He felt the way a fly caught in a spider's web must feel. This man gave him the creeps.

"It seems to me," said Nathan Chance, "that you're no different from every other kid, sponging off his parents. That's why I don't have kids. People say kids are worth their weight in gold, but I've never met one like that."

Trixie let out a nervous laugh. "You don't mean that," she said.

"I sure do," said Nathan. "Kids and dogs," he said, staring hard at Miss Precious. "Both of them are a waste of space."

"Just you wait," said Trixie, who wanted Nathan to be impressed with Billy. "He's got friends in high places. Go on, honey, don't be shy. Tell Nat about Walter Minks Junior."

Billy jumped back as Nathan moved over towards him as fast and as silently as a spider. He looked hard at Billy.

"Are we talking about Walter Minks the Third's son Walter?" he said.

"Yes," said Trixie, pleased to see Nathan was paying attention.

"How do you know Walter?" said Nathan, taking off his shades to look more closely at Billy. He had small eyes that seemed to look straight through you. Billy felt his insides go wobbly.

"Go on," said Dad, "tell Mr Chance how you came to meet Walter."

Billy was quiet.

"I'll tell you," said Trixie. "Billy met him on the plane. He lives in the Dakota Building. He has a driver and he is well loaded."

"Interesting," said Nathan, putting his shades back on. "Haven't you got work to do, Tony?" he went on. "Better let cowgirl here take Billy home."

"Sorry," said Dad when he and Billy came out of Nathan's office. "You'll have to run along with Trixie. I've a lot of work on at the moment, but I'll make it up to you later. You do understand, don't you?"

16

The day before her birthday party, Mighty Mamma and Billy were having breakfast together. The TV was on in the background. Neither of them was paying much attention to it. Then a picture of Walter flashed up on the screen.

"The headlines this hour ... " said the presenter. "Walter Minks Junior has been kidnapped. The ten-year-old son of Marilyn Tinsel and the multi-millionaire newspaper tycoon Walter Minks the Third was kidnapped last night outside the Dakota

Building where he was staying with his father."

Billy and Mighty Mamma stopped eating and stared at the TV.

"Walter Minks the Third," the presenter went on, "personally handed over the sum of three million dollars in the early hours of this morning and was assured that his son would be released at eight o'clock. So far there has been no sign of the child, and there has been no further communication from the kidnappers."

"This is terrible," said Mighty Mamma. "It gives me shivers in my bones to think that there are such nasty people in the world. Who would dream of doing that to a child?"

"This is really gross," said Billy. "Walter will be so frightened. What's going to happen to him?"

The doorbell rang and Billy went to open it. Trixie walked in, looking ghastly.

"I haven't slept a wink," she said. "I'm

afraid that Tony is in big trouble and the worst thing is, he don't know it."

"Sit down, Trixie," said Mighty Mamma. "You are making no sense."

There was a loud yelp as Trixie sat down on Miss Precious. "Oh sorry, honey," she said, lifting the dog up and giving it a kiss.

"This must be serious," said Billy to Mighty Mamma. "Look, Miss Precious isn't wearing any clothes."

"OK, Trixie," said Mighty Mamma, "why don't you tell us nice and slowly what's going on."

"Yesterday," said Trixie, "Nathan sent my Tony to Chicago to see the factory where the wagons are being made."

"So what's wrong with that?" said Mighty Mamma.

"Well, Tony calls me to say he's in Chicago and he just can't find the joint. I phoned Nathan to see if Tony has the right address. Well, I call and call. No answer, so I go round to the office. Now this is the strange part. There is no more office. It's all closed up. I can't get in because the locks have been changed and no one in the building knows anything."

Miss Precious started yelping.

"Oh, quiet, baby," said Trixie. "I tell you, that got me thinking. It's hard for me to say this, but I think that there are no wagons being made. I think Nathan has had Tony selling vacations that don't exist."

"If you are right, Tony is in big trouble," said Mighty Mamma.

"We could go to the police," said Billy.

"I will phone that nice detective Billy and I met," said Mighty Mamma. "He'll be able to help us."

"No," said Trixie, standing up, "you mustn't do that, Mrs Piccoloni."

"Why not?"

"Because I think everything has just got a whole lot worse. I think my boss, Nathan Chance, has kidnapped Walter."

"That's ridiculous," said Mighty Mamma. "What has your boss got to do with it?"

"It's just a feeling me and Miss Precious have in our bones. It's like the puzzles I do. It's all fitting together," said Trixie. "Alarm bells started to ring when I spilled the beans about Walter and the Dakota Building and everything. I just wanted him to be impressed with Tony's boy. I was so stupid to say that Billy knows Walter because if you think about it he's the perfect kid to kidnap."

"I bet it was him," said Billy. "He was like a spider. He gave me the creeps."

"I've always known that Nathan is one to take a chance," Trixie went on. "It's easy for him to clean up with all the money and lay the blame on Tony. Tony ain't smart with figures, you know."

Mighty Mamma and Billy sat down. Neither of them said a word.

"I can't get hold of Tony," said Trixie. "And I am sure worried about Walter. I mean, Nathan Chance doesn't like kids or dogs. He said so, didn't he?"

Billy nodded and Miss Precious yapped loudly. "You agree with me that we got to do something?"

"I still think we should call Detective Sherman," said Mighty Mamma.

"Wait," said Billy. "I have an idea."

94

Billy put the money-box on top of the TV
and turned it on. The presenter was saying,
"There is still no news on the whereabouts
of Walter Minks, the child kidnapped
yesterday. For the latest on the story we are
going over live to LA and to Walter Minks's
mother, Marilyn Tinsel." The camera focused
on a very beautiful weeping woman. Her
husband stood next to her.

"How do you feel?" said the reporter.

"My wife is too upset to speak," said the man. "That kid meant the world to us. We are flying to New York immediately. The police think he is still being held somewhere in the city, even though the ransom money has been paid."

"I just want my boy back. I'd give up all my fame to have him back," said Marilyn Tinsel tearfully. She was led away by her husband.

"That poor boy," said Mighty Mamma. "Where can he be? Finding him in this town is going to be like looking for a needle in a haystack."

"Do you think my money-box can help?" said Billy.

"Let's try it, Billy." And Mighty Mamma handed Billy two dimes.

Billy looked at Trixie. "You promise you won't tell a soul about this."

"I don't know what I'm promising but

OK, I promise," said Trixie.

The money-box stuck out its tongue. The first dime went clink and the money-box rubbed its chubby tummy.

"Oh, isn't that so cute!" said Trixie.

"Shhh," said Billy and Mighty Mamma together.

Now the money-box held out its hand for the second dime, threw it into its mouth and said, "Seven." Billy wrote the number down. Then it said, slightly slurring its words, "23." There was another longer pause after which it said slowly "14," followed by "3" and then "302." They all waited but the money-box had no more numbers to give. Billy quickly turned it off.

"I think it's running out of power," he said sadly.

"I get it," said Trixie, "the money-box gave you the numbers for the cake and the safe."

"Yes," said Billy, "but it also gave us some numbers that didn't mean anything."

"Give me the numbers you just wrote down, kid," said Trixie. And to Mighty Mamma's and Billy's complete surprise, she suddenly gave a whoop!

"I know! The kid's hidden somewhere in New York, right, but where? How do we find the location? Your money-box numbers give us the lead. Look." She produced a map of New York. "First of all, seven. We'll go to Seventh Avenue. Now," she said, following the route with her finger, "we'll cross at 23rd Street and look for number 14. If it's a hotel, 3 will mean the third floor and the last three numbers could mean the room. OK, Room 302!"

"What are we waiting for?" shouted Mighty Mamma, grabbing her coat and handbag. "Come on, and don't forget to bring the money-box with you, Billy."

They flagged down a yellow cab which screeched through the streets of New York and pulled up outside a run-down hotel.

A coachload of Italian tourists were checking in. Suitcases and arguments were cluttering up the lobby so that it was easy for them to slip unnoticed into an elevator and press the button for the third floor.

A long straight corridor with doors on either side led off the lobby. A linen trolley was parked halfway up it but there was no one in sight. Room 302 was near a flight of stairs.

"What now?" said Billy.

Mighty Mamma walked back to the trolley and took some clean towels off it.

"You stay here with Billy out of sight,"

she said to Trixie. "I'll go and see who's in there. Then if the money-box has got it right, we call Detective Sherman."

Mighty Mamma knocked on the door of Room 302. "Housekeeper!" she announced. Nothing happened. She knocked again. Finally a tough-looking man opened the door.

"What do you want?" said the man rudely. "Can't you read the sign? Do not disturb."

"Scusi," said Mighty Mamma, "but I have a job to do and someone asked for clean towels."

"Boss, did you order clean towels?" called the man.

"No, Sharky, I did not," came a voice that both Billy and Trixie recognised at once. So did little Miss Precious, who leapt out of Trixie's arms and ran yapping past Mighty Mamma, straight at the legs of Nathan Chance. What happened next happened so fast that neither Mighty Mamma nor Trixie had time to work out what they were doing. They just acted.

Taking aim, Mighty Mamma brought her handbag down hard on the head of Sharky, who went down like a boxer in the ring, out cold.

Miss Precious still had her teeth firmly in Nathan Chance's leg. Trixie rushed to help.

"Take that, you creep!" she shouted, giving Nathan a good biff. He reeled and was about to bash her back when Mighty Mamma gave him a knockout blow with her handbag. Nathan tottered, wobbling from side to side, and then crashed down on top of Sharky.

Billy pushed past them both and found Walter tied up in the bedroom.

"Wow, am I glad to see you! How did you know I was here?" said Walter.

"It's a long story," said Billy, untying him. "Are you all right?"

"Yes," said a very relieved Walter. "I thought I wasn't going to get out alive. That man was a really nasty piece of work."

"I know," said Billy.

"Tell me how you found me," said Walter.

"It was the money-box," said Billy.

"No," said Walter. "Really? That's amazing."

18

Detective Jack Sherman couldn't have been
more surprised by the sight that greeted
him as he entered Room 302. There were
little Mrs Piccoloni and a lady he had never
seen before, sitting on top of two large
men while a small dog ran yapping round
them. On the bed sat Walter and Billy
drinking cola. They were all talking away
as if it were a party.

"Hey!" said Detective Sherman, who was more than delighted to see that Walter was safe. "Sorry to interrupt you, but would someone care to tell me what's going on?"

It was Mighty Mamma who told the detective the story, while Trixie filled in the titbits.

"That's bad," said Walter when he heard that Billy's dad worked for Nathan Chance.

"The thing is," said Trixie, "Tony didn't know what Nathan was up to. He thought Nathan was interested in his Wild West Wagon Trail Tours, nothing else. And I didn't know what was going on either. Although I used to type his letters and answer the phone, he would never let me look at the files."

Detective Sherman listened attentively. Then he asked Walter, "Are you OK?"

"Yes, I'm just so pleased Billy found me."

"So am I," said Detective Sherman, leaning down to get a closer look at the two men lying on the floor. "You're under arrest," he said, clapping on the handcuffs and pulling them to their feet. When he saw Nathan Chance's face, he smiled. "Well, well," he said. "What have we got here? If it isn't Spike the Spider!"

"Spike the Spider!" shrieked Trixie. "Do you mean I've been working for Spike the Spider?"

"Call my lawyer," said Nathan. "You won't be able to prove a thing."

"He can't be Spike the Spider, Detective Sherman," said Billy. "He's Nathan Chance, Trixie's boss. He's the man who . . . "

"Billy," said Detective Sherman, "this is none other than the fraudster Spike the Spider, alias Nathan Chance, and I've been after him for a long time. I've never been able to pin anything on him because he always manages to do a runner, leaving someone else to take the blame."

"You ain't got no proof," snarled Spike

the Spider, standing unsteadily on his feet. "If you want to know where your money is, you'd better ask Tony Piccoloni. I can tell you," he said, looking at Billy, "your dad is well and truly trapped in my web."

"Tony ain't got no three million dollars!" shrieked Trixie. "You think I'd be working for this creep if he had three million dollars?"

"Calm down, lady," said Detective Sherman. "I think we all need to go down to the precinct."

"Tony," said Mighty Mamma, "he is what you might describe as more of a child than Billy here. He may be stupid but he wouldn't knowingly be involved in anything criminal."

"That's right," said Trixie. "I can vouch for that."

"Mrs Piccoloni," said Detective Sherman kindly, "I am sure what you are saying is the truth, but it doesn't look good."

"Please," said Billy. "If we could find the

money, would that help?"

Detective Sherman sighed. "It would be a start."

"The money-box!" shouted Walter excitedly. Then he said, "Oh sorry, Billy. I shouldn't have said that."

"What?" said Detective Sherman.

"I found Walter because of my money-box," said Billy. "It gave me the numbers and Trixie worked out what they meant. That's how we're here. Maybe it could find out where the money is hidden."

Detective Sherman looked at Billy. "OK, I owe you one for getting that safe open. Go on, kid, get the money-box and let's see what it comes up with."

Billy placed the money-box on the table. He put one dime on the tongue. It moved slowly and there was a dull clink as it swallowed the dime. Then, even more slowly, it rubbed its tummy and held out its hand.

The second coin just made it into the mouth. Then there was a silence that seemed to go on forever.

Just when they all thought the money-box would never say anything ever again, it began to speak. Very, very slowly it said, "Forty-five." Then it said, "45 6 245," and then the money-box's smiling mouth shut tight.

"Do it again," said Detective Sherman, disappointed. "I don't think those numbers mean anything."

Billy tried again, but the money-box's smiling mouth was firmly shut. "I think it's run out of batteries," said Billy.

"I think we'd all better get down to the precinct and get Walter reunited with his parents," said the detective.

"Wait please," said Walter. "What's important on 45th Street?"

"It's a long street, honey," said Trixie, looking disappointed.

"If my memory serves me right," said

Detective Sherman, "on the corner of 45th Street and 6th Avenue there's Mini Apple Storage."

"That's it!" cried Trixie. "Me and Miss Precious are sure that's it!"

"That's what?" said Billy.

"The last number could be a storage unit, honey," said Trixie.

"Come on, everyone, what are we waiting for?" said Detective Sherman.

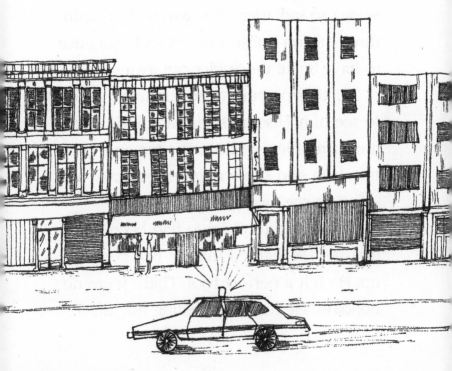

19

When they first arrived at Mini Apple
Storage it hadn't looked all that promising.
One sad old sofa was all there was in
lockup 245, and nothing else. According to
the guy on the desk it had just been
delivered that morning.

In the end it turned out that that old sofa
wasn't so sad after all. It was stuffed with
three million dollars and enough evidence
to have Spike the Spider put away for good.

Walter's parents were genuinely thrilled
to see him. His dad said that all his money
meant nothing without Walter, and even
his mum said she was going to make a real
effort to see more of him.

Tony's trip to Chicago had been a
disaster. He realised that he had been set
up. He felt a perfect fool. There were no
holidays. He had been selling hot air. A

very unhappy Tony Pickles made his way to the precinct to give himself up. The Chicago police questioned him for hours before they let him go, but the information he gave them was what they needed. They told Tony he was the wrong man in the wrong place at the wrong time.

"I'm sorry," he said to Billy when they were reunited, "I've made a mess of everything. But I promise you, kid, I'm going to turn over a new leaf."

"I don't understand why you left Mum and me to come here in the first place," said Billy.

"I don't understand it myself. I'd got myself into so much trouble with the money I owed, I suppose I thought it would be easier to start again. I had dreams of making it big like Frank Sinatra and then giving your mum back the money I lost."

"Why did you give me a money-box?" asked Billy.

"I sent away for it from a catalogue. I wanted you to be better with money than I am. I know you think I should have stayed with your mum, but I couldn't. I'm so sorry," said Dad. "I wanted to live life my way and it all went wrong."

"What about Trixie?" said Billy.

"You don't like her, do you?" said Dad.

Billy put his arms round him.

"Guess what," said Billy, "I like Trixie very much. I even quite like Miss Precious."

"You're a good boy, Billy. What did I do to deserve such a great boy as you?"

Billy shrugged his shoulders and put on a clown face, and Dad started to laugh.

Mighty Mamma's seventieth birthday party was a huge success. Detective

Sherman came with his family. Katy Gee showed up. Walter was there with his dad, though his mother had to fly back for a film she was making.

"But you know what," said Walter to Billy, "at least they're speaking. I mean, before they couldn't even be in a room together unless their lawyers were present." Billy laughed.

Santo had made an ice-cream cake shaped like the Statue of Liberty and afterwards there was dancing.

"Mrs Piccoloni," said Detective Sherman as he whirled Mighty Mamma across the floor, "there is one thing I would like to ask you. How did such a delicate lady as yourself manage to knock out two hardened criminals with a handbag?"

Mighty Mamma laughed out loud.
"I always keep a paperweight in it. You
never know who you might bump into."

At midnight they all sang Happy Birthday
and raised their glasses to Mighty Mamma.

She climbed up onto the platform with
the orchestra and, surrounded by her
family, thanked all the guests for coming.

"This has been a wonderful trip," said
Mighty Mamma. "I met my grandson Billy
for the first time and I love this city. There
is only one thing more to say. Tony, over
to you."

She looked at Billy's dad who grabbed
the microphone and belted out his
favourite Frank Sinatra song: "New York!
New York!"

20

The thing about adventure is that it is very hard to get back to normal when it's all over. Billy was thrilled to see Mum again and to tell her about what had happened to him and his famous money-box, but after a week the excitement of being back wore off.

Home seemed rather grey and drab after New York. Everything was just the same as it had always been: nothing had changed. Mum still worked too hard and her lady customers still complained about having their hair done in a barber's chair.

It was, thought Billy, as though he had never been away. The money-box sat on the window-sill again with two dimes beside it, a reminder of his last day with Dad when they had gone off together in search of the battery seller.

Much to their delight they had found him. But when Billy asked for Double B batteries the man smiled and said, "Kid, I never had no Double B batteries. Long life or short life, there ain't no such thing."

Dad wrote to Billy every week now. In his last letter, he had said that he had a steady job working with Santo in the café and that Trixie sent her love.

Billy and Walter talked a lot on the phone. Walter was very keen for Billy to come out next summer to spend time with him and his dad. "Things really are better," said Walter. "When I went to stay with my mum she took four days off filming just to spend time with me. It was great."

"It's hard," said Mum one Saturday afternoon after Billy had got off the phone and was looking down in the dumps. "You miss Dad and Trixie and Mighty Mamma and Santo, don't you?"

"No," said Billy untruthfully.

"Don't be daft, Billy. Of course you do. It's only normal."

"I love being here with you. It's just that I wish that they weren't so far away. It costs so much money to see them," said Billy sadly.

"I know, love. I wish there was something we could do about it but we just can't afford the fares."

"Do you mind about Trixie?" said Billy.

He hadn't asked his mum that question before.

"No," said Mum. "The best thing that happened between your dad and me was you. I'm happier on my own. He can't help being as daft as a Bakewell tart." They both laughed.

The radio was on in the background. "It's a rollover on the Lotto this week," said the announcer.

"You know, Mum," said Billy. "I've been thinking about those numbers the money-box gave me in New York. You know, the numbers that didn't mean anything."

"What about them?" said Mum.

"Well, I think we should give them a try. Maybe they were meant for when I got home."

"Can you remember what they were?" said Mum.

"There were seven of them," said Billy. "And I wrote them down. Let me find my notebook. Look — 26, 34, 12, 19, 21, 7, 3."

"Well then, Billy Pickles," said Mum, "I think, with seven numbers and it being a Saturday, that we should buy a lottery ticket."

21

That evening, they were sitting in front of the TV with their fish and chips on their laps waiting for the lottery numbers to come up.

"Ladies and gentlemen, it's a rollover," said the TV presenter, "and here comes the first ball — number 26!"

Billy felt the hairs on the back of his neck stand up and he knew, as he watched first one then another ball come rolling down, that their lives were about to change.

"Number 34! Number 12! Number 19! Number 21! Number 7! And here comes the Bonus Ball," shouted the presenter.

Billy watched as the final ball, Number 3, slid into view.

Mum leapt up and shouted for joy. She and Billy danced round the room.

"We've won!" she cried. "The money-box has come up trumps. I can have a proper hairdressing salon. We can buy a house of our own. We can go on holiday to Italy and visit Mighty Mamma. Oh Billy," said Mum, tears of joy running down her cheeks, "what do you say?"

"I say," said Billy, with the biggest grin ever on his face, "I say our number has come up, and this time, Mum, it really is the right one."

More  Stories

The Strongest Girl in the World

Josie Jenkins, aged eight and three quarters, is good at doing tricks, but she amazes herself and everyone else with her strength when she lifts a table, a car, and even a bus with no effort at all. Mr Two Suit promises to bring her fame and fortune – and so he does. But when Josie and her mum and dad and brother Louis are flown to New York and she becomes a celebrity, she finds that she has to cope with all kinds of ups and downs.

The Smallest Girl Ever

Everyone expects Ruby Genie to have the same fantastic magical powers as her famous parents did. But Ruby can't do any magic at all. Or so she thinks. Then Ruby begins to get smaller... and smaller. And she discovers that even though she is so tiny she can fit into a handbag, she can still be clever and brave and find people to love her.

The Boy Who Could Fly

One day the Fat Fairy turns up at Thomas Top's house to grant him a birthday wish. Thomas can't think what to ask for, so he wishes he could fly. That's how Thomas goes from being just an ordinary boy whom no one notices to being the most popular boy in the school. But it makes him sad that grown-ups can't see the wonderful things he can do – especially his dad.

The Invisible Boy

Sam's parents have got lost on a trip to the moon and he has been left in the care of the horrible Hilda Hardbottom. Everything seems hopeless. But one night he notices a tiny spaceship in the cabbage patch. Out of it steps a little alien called Splodge. Splodge is a great new friend for him – especially since he knows how to make Sam invisible.

How Sam uses his invisibility to scare the pants off Hilda Hardbottom, and how he finds that being braver makes better, is a wonderful story and a very funny one.